Lucy the Poorly Puppy

Lucy the Poorly Puppy

Holly Webb

Illustrated by Sophy Williams

stripes

For William and Robin

STRIPES PUBLISHING
An imprint of Magi Publications
1 The Coda Centre, 189 Munster Road,
London SW6 6AW

A paperback original
First published in Great Britain in 2011

ISBN: 978-1-84715-152-0

A CIP catalogue record for this book is available
from the British Library.

Printed and bound in the UK.

10 9 8 7 6 5 4 3 2 1

Chapter One

"Bella's looking so fat!" Lauren peered under the kitchen table at Bella, the family's beagle. She was sitting in amongst everyone's feet, panting and looking rather uncomfortable. Her tummy was huge, and the expression on her face was a bit grumpy.

Dad checked under the table too. "Well, she is due to have the pups any day now. I'll take her temperature later on, to check if it's gone down."

Lauren nodded. They had been taking Bella's temperature every day for the last couple of weeks, as their vet, Mark, had told them it was the best way to tell if the puppies were about to come.

Bella padded heavily out from under the table, and wandered over to her cushion. She took hold of the edge in her teeth – it was a big, soft cushion, made of red fabric – and tugged it closer to the radiator. Then she nudged it with her nose, this way and that, as though she couldn't get it quite how she wanted it.

Lauren watched her hopefully. "Does that look like nesting to you?" she asked.

"I don't know. It might be..." her mum said doubtfully. It was the first time Bella had had puppies, and they were having to learn as they went along, even though Lauren's mum had bought three different books on dog breeding.

"We need to set off for school," Dad pointed out, checking his watch.

Lauren sighed. "I bet Bella has the puppies while I'm at school, and I really, really want to be there. Couldn't I just stay at home? It's the last day of term, we're not going to actually do anything, are we?"

Mum shook her head. "No. Besides, don't you want to say goodbye to all your friends? You won't see most of them for the next six weeks, remember."

Lauren frowned. It was true. She loved living way out in the country. Their home had been a farmhouse originally, and it had a huge garden. The old cowsheds had been made into her parents' office, and there was a barn across the yard that Lauren could play in. But there were bad things about it too. She lived twenty minutes' drive from the village where her school was, and her best friend Millie lived in a village that was about twenty minutes' beyond the school! So arranging to see Millie in the holidays always meant lots of planning.

Lauren fetched her bag and the present she'd got for her teacher, Miss Ford, and took one last look at Bella on the way out of the kitchen door. The beautiful brown and white dog was squirming around on her cushion as though she couldn't quite get comfy.

"Can you just hold on until I get home?" Lauren pleaded. But Bella looked up at her with big, mournful eyes. Lauren stroked her lovingly. "I see what you mean. You must really want to be back to your old self again. If it happens today, good luck, Bella. It'll be worth it, you're going to have gorgeous puppies soon."

"She's going to be very tired," Dad pointed out. "We'll have to look after her. I remember doing all this with Rusty, my parents' dog, when I was just a bit older than you. Now come on, Lauren, we're going to be late."

As they were bumping down the lane in the car towards the main road, Lauren asked, "How many puppies do you think Bella will have?"

Dad shook his head. "Hard to tell – could be anything from one to fourteen, according to those books your mum bought. Rusty only had five."

Lauren frowned. "It can't just be one. Bella's enormous."

"I think you're probably right – she is very big. I'd say we're looking at quite a few," Dad agreed.

He sighed as he noted her sparkling eyes and excited smile. "Lauren…"

"What is it?" Lauren looked over at him worriedly.

"Sweetheart, just remember that we aren't keeping these puppies. They're all going to go to new homes."

Lauren hesitated for a moment. "I know," she said quietly. She was silent for a little while and then added, "But we'll have them for a couple of months, won't we? That's all the summer holidays to play with them, and more."

Dad nodded. "Exactly. Of course we'll miss them when they go, but it'll be easier if we remember that they aren't ours to keep."

"I won't forget," Lauren promised. "Oh, there's Millie, Dad! Can you let me out here? I can walk up the road to school with her and her mum, can't I?"

Dad pulled up, and Lauren jumped out of the car, waving to her best friend.

"Hi! How's Bella? Have the puppies arrived yet?" Millie asked breathlessly.

Lauren shook her head, then smiled. "Bella was being really funny this morning. She kept messing around with her bed as if she was nesting. There might even be puppies when I get home!" she said, swinging her school bag excitedly.

"You're so lucky," said Millie. "Mum, can we have one of Bella's puppies? Pleeeease?"

"Oh, Millie, you know I'd love one," said her mum, hitching Millie's baby sister Amy higher up on her hip. "But it just wouldn't be fair to have a dog – I'm busy with your sister, and your dad's at work during the day. A puppy would get lonely."

Millie sighed. "I suppose so."

"You'll be able to play with them when you come round in the holidays," Lauren promised her. "And I won't get to keep the puppies either. Dad was reminding me in the car."

Millie nodded. "Still, you'll have weeks and weeks to play with them all. Oh, there's the bell. See you later, Mum!"

The two girls ran into class, and joined the crowd of children round Miss Ford, all begging her to open their goodbye present first.

Chapter Two

Lauren usually spent ages chatting to all her friends at the end of school, but today she was desperate to see if the puppies had arrived. She dashed out into the playground to find Dad waiting by the gate. Millie chased after her.

"Has Bella had the puppies yet?" Lauren gasped. She'd been running so fast she had to grab on to Dad's arm to stop herself falling over.

Dad steadied her, laughing. "Yes."

"How many?" Lauren squeaked excitedly.

Dad smiled. "Guess."

Lauren frowned. "Five?"

"Nowhere near. Ten!"

"Ten puppies?" Lauren turned round to Millie, her eyes round with amazement. "Ten? That's a *huge* litter!"

Millie laughed. "You'll have to think of ten names!"

"That's going to be tricky," Dad said. Lauren gave him a worried look. He didn't sound quite as happy as she thought the owner of ten puppies should. A sudden horrible thought hit her. Ten puppies was loads – it must have been such hard work for Bella, giving birth to so many. What if something was wrong with her? Lauren opened her mouth to ask, and then shut it again. She didn't want to talk about something so scary in the middle of the school playground.

Instead, she hugged Millie goodbye, and promised to email her a picture of the puppies later.

But as soon as she and Dad were heading for the car, she grabbed his hand. "Dad, is everything OK?"

"What do you mean?" Dad looked at her carefully.

"I just thought you seemed a bit worried – after you told us there were so many puppies. Is Bella all right?"

Dad gave her a hug. "Bella's fine. I mean, she's exhausted, but she did really well. It's not Bella..." He hesitated. "Lauren, one of the puppies is a lot smaller than the others. Mum and I – we're not sure this one will make it. It's such a tiny scrap of a thing, and when it was first born, we weren't even sure if it was breathing. Bella had another puppy straight after, and she didn't have time to lick the little puppy like she did with the others, or bite through its cord. I had to cut the cord myself, and I rubbed the little pup with a flannel to bring it round." He shook his head. "It did start to breathe, but it's not as strong as the other puppies, not by a long way."

"Do you think it might die, Dad?" Lauren whispered.

Dad sighed. "I hope not – but we have to face the fact that it might."

"That's so sad." Lauren felt tears stinging her eyes. The poor little puppy.

"Nine healthy puppies is a great litter," Dad reminded her.

Lauren nodded. "I guess so. But I can't help worrying about the little one."

"I know, me too. Still, it might perk up. You never know."

Lauren crossed her fingers behind her back. She wanted Bella to have all ten of her wonderful puppies safe and well.

Lauren crept in the kitchen door. She was trying very hard not to upset Bella.

But Bella looked like she'd be impossible to disturb. She was stretched flat out on her side, fast asleep on the pile of old towels that Mum had put aside for her and the puppies to sleep on, in the special low wooden pen Dad had made for them. They'd been worried that the puppies might fall off Bella's big cushion.

The puppies were all snuggled up next to their mum, fast asleep in a pile of heads and paws. Lauren knelt down beside the pen and tried to count them, but she couldn't work out where one pup ended and the next began.

She couldn't see which was the one that Dad was worried about, either.

"They're so tiny!" she whispered to Mum.

"I know, aren't they beautiful?" Mum beamed.

Lauren frowned. "They're all black and white! I can hardly see any brown on them at all. That's really weird, when Bella's brown and white."

Mum shook her head. "I thought that, but then I looked it up in our beagle book, and it says they're usually born mostly black and white. The black might change to brown over the next few weeks, or stay as it is. Most beagles are black and white with brown patches – tricolour, it's called. Bella's quite rare, being all brown and white."

"Look how pink their noses are," Lauren breathed. "And I can hear them snuffling! They're so gorgeous."

"Aren't they?" Dad agreed. "Oh, look, Bella's waking up."

Lauren watched Bella yawn and blink sleepily, and crouched closer to the pen, expecting Bella to want to lick her hand. She was such a friendly dog, and she loved to cuddle up with Lauren

– preferably on the sofa watching cartoons.

But today Bella seemed not to see her. She was only interested in her puppies. She nudged them awake, pushing them gently towards her tummy so they could start feeding.

"She was like that with me too," Mum murmured. "Not interested. It's as if she's only got eyes for her puppies now." She put her arm round Lauren's shoulders. "Don't worry. She'll only be like this for the first couple of weeks, until they open their eyes and start to move around. Then they won't need her so much, and she'll be our sweet Bella again."

Lauren nodded. "Can I pick up one of the puppies?" she asked. "Will Bella let us?"

"We haven't touched them yet," Dad said. "We didn't want to upset Bella."

Lauren peered at the pile of puppies, as Bella woke them up. "Which is the little one – the one that was having trouble breathing properly?" she asked anxiously. "Oh! I think I can see – is it the one Bella's licking?"

Mum nodded. "Yes, that one's definitely a lot smaller than the others."

"Oh, look, you can see its little brown eyebrows!" Lauren said admiringly.

She edged closer to the pen, and Bella glanced up, as if to check that she wasn't going to harm the puppies. Lauren shuffled back a little, and Bella quickly went back to licking and nudging at the tiny puppy. The others were all feeding already – Lauren could hear the strange, wheezy squeak as they sucked. She giggled. "Look, Mum, that puppy's sitting on the other one's head!"

Mum smiled. "I don't think they mind as long as they're getting their mum's milk."

Dad was looking at one of the others. "Hey, pup. I don't think that's going to do you much good," he chuckled. "Look, that big puppy's trying to suck Bella's paw."

Bella looked round at the sound of Dad's voice, and spotted the confused puppy. She wrinkled her nose, and then gently pushed the puppy over to her tummy to feed with its brothers and sisters. Then she went back to trying to rouse the tiny pup.

"That one really is loads smaller than the others," Lauren said worriedly.

"And it's going to stay that way if it doesn't feed," Dad put in. "Oh, hang on though, look. Bella's got it moving."

The littlest puppy scrabbled wearily, its paws waving. It was making sad squeaking sounds, as though it wished Bella had left it to sleep, but at last it managed to burrow in among the rest of the litter.

"Is it feeding?" Mum asked hopefully.

"I think so." Lauren tried to listen for sucking sounds, but it was hard to tell with nine other puppies feeding at the same time. "Its head's moving backwards and forwards, like the others."

Dad nodded. "That's good, I was getting worried."

Then Lauren winced as one of the other puppies kicked the tiny one in the stomach – not on purpose, the bigger puppy was just scrambling to get back to Bella's milk. The tiny puppy lay there, kicking feebly, and then it seemed to go back to sleep. Lauren watched anxiously, willing it to wake up and feed again. But the littlest puppy just lay where it was, while its brothers and sisters wriggled and kicked for the best spot.

Chapter Three

Hi Millie,

Here's a photo of the newborn puppies! I bet you can't count all ten in this picture, though, they're all squeezed up together. They're really gorgeous, but there's one tiny one that won't feed properly from Bella. I just hope it's going to get better. Please come and see the puppies soon.

Love Lauren x

Lauren sent her email to Millie, and went downstairs to find Dad making the dinner and Mum cuddling one of the puppies, while Bella sat at the edge of the pen and kept a close eye on her.

"Oh, wow, she let you pick one up!"

Mum nodded. "But I was very careful. I washed my hands, and then I stroked Bella first, so that I didn't make the puppy smell like me. The book I was reading said that it was good to start handling puppies early, to get them used to people, but I don't want to worry Bella. She doesn't seem too bothered, though – we thought she would be OK, as she's such a friendly dog." Mum ran her finger very gently down the snoozing puppy's back. "If you wash your hands, you can stroke the puppy, too."

Lauren carefully washed her hands, and made a fuss of Bella first, stroking her with both hands to get Bella's scent on her fingers. Then she stroked the puppy with one finger, like her mum had done. It felt like slightly damp velvet – and it was no bigger than one of the Beanie toy dogs she had on her windowsill upstairs. "It's so soft..." she breathed.

Bella made a little snorting noise, and lay down next to her puppies again, but she was still eyeing Lauren and her mum.

"Look how fat its tummy is," Mum pointed out. "This puppy's absolutely stuffed."

"I think we should put it back," Lauren said. "Bella looks a bit worried. But she hasn't growled or anything. She's such a good dog."

"And a good mother too," Dad said, from over by the cooker. "She's taken to it so well."

Lauren's mum gently slipped the puppy back into the pen next to Bella, who licked it all over. The puppy made a squeaking noise as Bella's big tongue licked its head, but it didn't wake up.

"Where's the tiny one?" Lauren asked, trying to count the puppies.

Mum frowned. "I'm sure I saw it just a moment ago, and I think it had some more milk, which is really good. Apparently Bella's milk is full of all sorts of good stuff on the day they're born. The puppies get all the benefit of the vaccinations she's had, that kind of thing."

"I can't see the little puppy now," Lauren muttered anxiously. "What if it's under all the others and they squash it?"

Mum knelt down next to her. "Isn't that it?" she asked, pointing to a puppy.

Lauren shook her head. "No, brown eyebrows, remember? That one's just black and white."

"Oh yes." Mum edged round to the other side of the pen. "It's here, look, behind Bella. It must have got pushed out of the way by the others."

Lauren followed her, moving slowly so as not to disturb Bella. "Is it OK?"

Bella was watching carefully, and as soon as she realized what had happened, she wriggled round and tried to nudge the puppy over with her nose. But the puppy was fast asleep and didn't move. Bella glanced up at Lauren and her mum, almost as though she wasn't quite sure what to do.

"Should we move the puppy for her?" Lauren asked, frowning.

Mum was starting to say, "Maybe we should…" when Bella leaned down and picked up the tiny puppy in her mouth.

"Mum, what's Bella doing?" Lauren whispered in horror.

"Don't worry," Mum soothed her. "It's fine. Dogs do that, Lauren, she won't hurt the puppy."

But it didn't look at all comfortable. The puppy's legs dangled out on either side of Bella's mouth, and it wheezed and squeaked unhappily. Bella swiftly tucked it in along the row of teats on her tummy, and watched hopefully.

Lauren and Mum watched too, and Dad left the pasta sauce he was stirring and came to peer over their shoulders, holding a tomatoey wooden spoon.

"It's feeding," Lauren whispered excitedly, seeing the little shoulders moving.

Mum nodded. "And as all the others are asleep, hopefully it'll be able to keep feeding for a while."

"Oh, that's good." Dad sighed with relief. "And good timing. Dinner's ready."

Lauren went to bed that night very reluctantly. She wanted to stay and watch the puppies, especially the tiniest one. She was still worried that it wasn't getting enough milk. Because it wasn't as big as the others, it couldn't wriggle its way back to Bella's teats when it got pushed away, like the others could. Instead of barging past its brothers and sisters, the littlest puppy would just whine miserably and go back to sleep.

"Can't I stay up a bit longer? It's the first day of the holidays tomorrow," Lauren begged.

"It's already an hour later than bedtime!" Mum pointed out. "You can come down early in the morning to see them. But now you need to go to bed."

Lauren sighed, recognizing Mum's no-argument voice. Still, she was sure she wouldn't ever sleep.

Lauren woke up suddenly, to find her bedroom in darkness. So she *had* fallen asleep after all.

She sat up, hugging her knees. What time was it? It felt like the middle of the night. She glanced at her luminous clock. Two o'clock in the morning. Lauren shuddered. No wonder it was so dark. She lay down again, but she didn't feel sleepy any more. Something was worrying her, and she wasn't sure what it was. Then she realized – the puppies! Of course, how could she have forgotten about them?

She couldn't hear any noise from downstairs. Bella and the puppies were probably fast asleep. But she couldn't stop worrying that something was wrong, and that was why she had woken up.

It wouldn't hurt to go and have a look, would it? Lauren smiled to herself – Mum had said she could come down early to see the puppies, after all. She probably hadn't meant quite this early, but still...

She got out of bed and crept over to her door, quickly pulling on her dressing gown. As she ran across the landing to the stairs, she could hear her dad snoring. She hurried down the stairs, and into the kitchen. She could make out little squeaks and sucking noises – the puppies were awake and feeding, but that wasn't really surprising. Lauren had been reading

Mum's puppy books, and it said that for the first couple of weeks they would need to feed every two hours.

Mum had left a small lamp from the living room plugged in on the counter, so Bella had a bit of light for feeding the puppies. Bella was lying on her side looking sleepy, but she thumped her tail gently on the floor of the pen as she saw Lauren.

"Hey, Bella. I just came to see how you all are," Lauren whispered, kneeling beside the pen.

Bella closed her eyes wearily, as Lauren patted her head and leaned over to count the puppies. Then she counted them again. Only nine!

Where was the little puppy with the brown eyebrows?

"Oh, Bella, where's it gone?" Lauren whispered, but Bella was half-asleep, and she only twitched her tail.

Lauren checked behind Bella, where the puppy had ended up before, but there was nothing there. She was sure the other puppies weren't lying on the little one, and it couldn't possibly have climbed out. Frantically, Lauren started to feel around the shadowy edges of the box.

"Oh!" Lauren gasped, as she touched something little and soft, pushed away in the corner. "There you are!" She picked up the puppy, waiting for it to squeak and complain, but it didn't make a sound. "Oh, no, I didn't wash my hands – I suppose it's too late now." Lauren lifted the puppy up to see better, and realized that it was saggy and cold in her hands.

"Oh no, please…" she murmured, and snuggled the puppy in a fold of her dressing gown. "Mum! Dad!" she yelled, as she raced back up the stairs. "We need to call the vet!"

Chapter Four

"It woke up a little bit while I was holding it," Lauren explained to Mark, the vet. "Is it going to be all right?"

Mark put away his stethoscope and looked at the puppy thoughtfully. "You did really well to catch her when you did, Lauren. She's a she, by the way."

Lauren smiled, just a little. She had thought the puppy was a she – it was something about those cute brown eyebrows.

"It looks to me like she was slipping away," Mark went on, gently stroking the puppy's head. "Puppies can't control how warm or cold they are, they need their mum to keep them warm. You cuddling her warmed her up again. The real problem is that she's not strong enough to feed properly by herself. But you could hand-rear her." He glanced up at Lauren, and her mum and dad. "I can't promise she'll make it. But it's worth a try. It's a lot of work, though."

Lauren's dad frowned. "What does hand-rearing mean, exactly? I've looked after puppies before, but I've never had to hand-rear one. Would we feed her with a bottle?"

"A baby's bottle?" Lauren asked, looking at the tiny puppy. She was about the same size as a baby's bottle!

Mark shook his head. "No, a special puppy one. I've got one somewhere." He rooted about in his bag. "Here it is. I nipped into the surgery when you called and picked up some puppy milk replacement, and some advice on hand-rearing." He handed Lauren's dad a jar of white powder, and a leaflet. "You mix it with water, just like baby formula. Puppies can't drink cows' milk, it's got the wrong mix of nutrients."

Lauren's dad read the instructions on the jar. "Every two hours?" he asked, sounding slightly worried.

"Only for the first week," Mark reassured him. "After that you'll

44

probably be able to leave her without a feed through the middle of the night."

Dad rubbed his eyes wearily – it was now four o'clock in the morning. He and Mum ran their own mail-order business from home, and he'd been up late checking orders. He nodded. "Well, that's what we'll do." He glanced at Mum, who was looking anxious. "We can't not," he added gently.

Mum nodded. "Of course. It's going to be hard though." She smiled at Lauren. "A bit like when you were little."

Mark smiled. "But puppies grow faster than babies. They stop drinking their mum's milk at about seven weeks old. This little one should be feeding herself before you know it."

Lauren nodded. If it worked… Mark hadn't sounded absolutely sure that it would. But Lauren had already saved this puppy once, and if it was anything to do with her, the little one was going to make it.

"I'll do it," she said to her parents. "The feeding, I mean. I don't mind."

"You can't get up every two hours in the middle of the night!" Mum said, sounding horrified.

Lauren went over to fill the kettle. "We should feed her now, shouldn't we? Do we have to use boiled water? Like Millie's mum uses for her little sister's bottles?"

Mark grinned at Lauren's parents. "It sounds like Lauren knows what she's doing."

Lauren beamed at him. She really wanted to help, but she had a feeling Mum and Dad weren't going to be keen. "Do we have to keep the puppy separate from the others?" she asked, trying hard to think of anything else they might need to know.

Mark frowned. "I would for tonight. She's obviously having trouble keeping warm, she'll need a box and a hot-water bottle. Look, the leaflet shows you.

But after tonight, she'd be better off staying with her mum and the rest of the puppies, if she can. Just take her out for her feeds. Best of luck, and if there's any problems, give the surgery a ring."

The boiled water took ages to cool down, and Lauren kept wanting to blow on it.

Mum went to prepare a box for Lucy, and Dad sat at the kitchen table reading the instruction leaflet Mark had left. "Small cardboard box. Blanket. Hot-water bottle," he muttered. "We should have thought about all of this before, but it just never crossed my mind that we'd have so many and Bella wouldn't be able to feed them all. Uuurrgh!"

"What?" Lauren turned round, still cradling the puppy.

Dad was making a face. "According to this leaflet, we're going to have to help the puppy poo… They don't do it themselves, apparently, so because Bella won't be licking her after she's fed, we'll have to wipe round her bottom with wet cotton wool."

Lauren made a face back. That *was* a bit yucky. But it didn't put her off. She was going to do anything she had to, to keep the puppy going. Even if that meant making her poo.

"I think this water's cool enough to mix the formula now. Not long till you can have some milk, Lucy."

"Lucy?" Mum asked. "When did you name her?"

Lauren looked up. "I didn't even notice I had! But don't you think she looks like her name's Lucy?"

Mum nodded, but she was frowning, and Lauren bit her lip. She had a horrible feeling that Mum hadn't wanted her to name the tiny puppy in case she didn't make it.

Lauren carefully spooned the powder into the bottle, and mixed in the water. "Wake up, little one… Does it say how to hold her, Dad?"

Her dad skimmed through the instructions. "Flat, on her tummy, not on her back like a human baby. Here, look, on a towel." He laid a towel over Lauren's knees, and Lauren set Lucy down on her tummy. Her paws splayed out and she scrabbled a little and let out a tiny squeak, unsure what was going on.

"It's OK." Lauren picked up the bottle, and gently put it against Lucy's mouth.

"Squeeze the bottle a little," Mum suggested. "She doesn't know what it is. Let her taste a few drops of the milk."

All of a sudden Lucy started to suck eagerly, as she tasted the milk in her mouth. Her tiny pink paws, with their little transparent claws, pattered against Lauren's fingers, making her giggle. "Wow, she was ready for that."

Lucy only took five minutes to down the bottle.

"Goodness, should we give her some more?" Mum asked.

Lauren shook her head. "No, this is how much Mark said for now. The tub of powder says how much you give for what size of puppy over a whole day, and then you have to divide that up between the feeds." She gave a big yawn, and on her knee, Lucy did the same.

Mum laughed. "I think we should all go to bed. Especially if we have to be up at six-thirty to feed her again."

Lauren looked up at her mum hopefully. "Mum, my bedroom's lovely and warm, and if I have her box in there, I can keep an eye on her…"

"But we have to feed her so early. You don't want to get up at half-past six in the holidays!" Dad smiled.

"I do, I really do!" Lauren promised. "I was the one who woke up and found her, Dad. I really want to help."

Dad looked over at Lauren's mum. "What do you think, Annie?"

Mum sighed. "I suppose so. But only for tonight, Lauren. Tomorrow, when she's a bit stronger, Lucy can go back with Bella and the other puppies."

Lauren nodded eagerly and picked up the cardboard box. Inside, Lucy was snuggling up against the well-wrapped hot-water bottle. She looked happier than she had all day, Lauren thought. She padded back up the stairs, yawning uncontrollably. She set the box down next to her bed, and fell asleep listening to the minute wheezy breaths from inside the box.

It was really hard to get up when Dad came in at half-past six, but Lauren dragged herself out of bed, and carried Lucy's box downstairs to watch Dad make up her next feed. The trip downstairs hadn't disturbed Lucy at all, she noticed with a smile. The puppy was still snoozing peacefully next to the cooling hot-water bottle.

In the kitchen, Bella was out of the puppy pen looking hungry, and Lauren fed her while Dad boiled the kettle.

"Can I feed Lucy again?" Lauren begged, and Dad handed her the bottle.

"You might as well – you certainly seemed to have the knack earlier!"

Going downstairs might not have

woken Lucy, but the smell of the puppy formula certainly did, and she was gasping and squeaking with excitement as soon as Lauren held the bottle to her mouth.

After she'd cleaned Lucy up, Lauren took her over to Bella. She and Dad hovered anxiously, not too close to the puppy pen, watching to see how Bella would react.

"I hope Lucy will be all right," Lauren muttered. "It said in that leaflet that sometimes the mum tries to lick the human smell away and accidentally hurts the puppy."

Dad put an arm round her shoulders. "We'll watch really carefully," he promised. "And it's not as if Bella's a dog at a big breeder's, who lives outside and doesn't really know people that well. She's part of our family. Hopefully our smell won't upset her too much."

"Look!" Lauren whispered.

Bella was sniffing thoughtfully at Lucy, and Lauren held her breath as Bella started to lick the little puppy. But Bella didn't look at all upset, just a little surprised.

Lauren giggled. "I think Bella's so worn out I bet she'd hardly noticed Lucy was gone!"

Over the next few days, Lauren was sure that Lucy had started to recognize her. If Lucy started squeaking in her box, she would calm down as soon as Lauren picked her up, but not if it was Mum or Dad. Lauren knew it was probably just that Lucy recognized her by smell as the person who usually fed her, but it still made her feel special. She couldn't wait for Lucy to open her eyes, so that the puppy could see her as well as smell her.

Mum and Dad were supposed to be taking it in turns to do the night feeds, but Lauren couldn't help waking up when she heard the alarm go off in their bedroom. And once she was awake, she just couldn't stay in bed. Mum even stopped telling her off about it by the end of their second night of puppy-rearing.

Lucy was putting on weight now,

although not as fast as the other puppies, who were fat and glossy-furred. She adored her feeds, but Lauren suspected she might always be a bit smaller than her brothers and sisters.

Lucy squeaked and sucked at Lauren's fingers as Lauren scooped her up. She knew Lauren's scent, and she was sure it was time for Lauren to feed her, and she was so, so hungry.

Lauren giggled as Lucy's little pink paws flailed around. "I'm just waiting for it to cool down. You don't want to burn your mouth!"

Lucy squeaked even louder. Where was the milk?

"OK, OK, here you go."

Lucy sighed happily, and settled down to sucking. That was much better.

After the first week, Lauren and her parents could leave Lucy for six hours in the middle of the night without a feed. Dad said he'd do the midnight feed on his own – he was used to staying up late working anyway. Lauren had to admit it was really nice to get a proper night's sleep again, even though she still had to get up super-early for Lucy's morning feed.

Millie came to visit the puppies when they were about two weeks old.

"Can I feed Lucy?" she asked hopefully. "That photo you sent me of you feeding her was so cute. She's even more gorgeous now her eyes are open, though."

"She is, isn't she?" Lauren agreed, handing Millie the bottle.

Lucy watched Lauren the whole time she was feeding, and Lauren could tell she was a bit confused why somebody else was holding her bottle.

"You have to burp her now, like your mum burps Amy!" Lauren told Millie, when Lucy had finished.

Now that the puppies were two weeks old, their eyes were open, although they still hadn't really started to move around much. The really exciting thing was that their markings were starting to come through. Lucy had more brown on her face now, not just her pretty eyebrows, and all the puppies were changing every day.

Even though the puppies were still too tiny to really play with, Millie didn't want to leave when her mum came to pick her up.

Lauren waved goodbye from the door, and sighed as Millie's car disappeared down the lane. She really missed seeing her best friend every day.

"Lauren, I've got some really exciting news," her mum started, as she came back into the kitchen. "Hey, what's the matter?"

"I just wish I could see Millie more often in the holidays, that's all. Email and phoning aren't the same as having a friend close by."

Her mum gave her a hug. "This is going to be extra-good news for you, then." She beamed at Lauren. "We've rented out the cottage. To a family with a boy the same age as you!"

Lauren blinked. The cottage was on

the other side of the orchard, just beyond the farmyard. The old tenant had left ages ago, and Lauren had forgotten they were trying to find someone new.

"He's called Sam Martin, and he's got a little sister called Molly. Isn't that wonderful? You'll have a friend really close by!"

Lauren nodded slowly, but she wasn't sure it was all that wonderful. What if she didn't like this boy? And even if she did, he wouldn't be as good a friend as Millie.

Chapter Five

"Oh, that sounds like the Martins at the door!" Mum fussed around the kitchen, putting the kettle on. "Would you open it, Lauren?"

It was two weeks after Mum had broken the news about the new neighbours moving in, and they'd said they were going to pop round that afternoon. Lauren still couldn't help wishing it was a girl her age rather than a boy. And she didn't want some strange boy and his little sister messing around with Lucy and upsetting her. Instead of opening the door, she quickly dashed upstairs with Lucy, and stashed her in the box she'd slept in on the first night. Mum still let her take Lucy upstairs occasionally, and Lucy couldn't get out of the box yet, although she really liked trying.

Lucy whined in surprise as Lauren put her down. What was happening? She had been having a nice cuddle, and now she was being left all on her own! She stood up with her paws against the edge of the box, scrabbling hard. Where was Lauren? She whimpered miserably.

Lauren ran back downstairs, and tried to look friendly as Mum introduced her to Nicky Martin and Sam, a blond-haired boy who looked just as embarrassed as she felt. Sam's dad was still sorting things out at the house, and his little sister was asleep, Nicky said.

Sam cuddled one of the puppies, the big boy that they had named Buster, and didn't really say much. Lauren was just hoping that they might go soon – surely they must have loads of unpacking to do? But then her mum nudged her, and said meaningfully, "Why don't you show Sam round the farm?"

Lauren frowned. It was nearly time to feed Lucy, and she didn't want to anyway!

Her mum glared at her, and she gave a tiny sigh and turned to Sam. "Come on, then. You can bring Buster, if you like."

Sam nodded, and followed her out into the yard. "He's really nice. Is he your favourite?"

Lauren shook her head.

"Don't you have a favourite? He'd be mine, he's great." Sam snuggled Buster up under his chin.

Lauren didn't know what to say.

It would sound stupid to admit she'd hidden Lucy away. "I like them all," she said, a bit vaguely.

Lauren trailed around the farm, showing Sam the orchard, and the old barn on the other side of the yard. There were a few bales of hay in it still, and she liked to hide out in there sometimes.

"This is cool. I bet the puppies would love it in here," said Sam.

Lauren nodded. "They haven't been outside much yet, but Dad's making a wire run so they can play in the orchard."

Sam looked up. "Oh, that's my mum calling. I suppose we have to go and unpack."

He handed Buster to Lauren, and they headed back to the farmhouse. Lauren supposed Sam was OK really – at least he liked the puppies – but she didn't think they were going to be best friends or anything, which was obviously what Mum was hoping.

"He was nice, wasn't he?" Mum asked, as they waved goodbye to Sam and his mum. "Gosh, look at Buster!" She tickled the puppy under the chin. "He's huge. I must see about putting an ad in the local paper about new homes for the puppies. And there are a couple of good puppy websites too."

Lauren swallowed. Her heart seemed to have suddenly jumped into her throat. New homes! She had almost forgotten about that – she had wanted to forget.

"But they're only a month old, Mum!" she cried.

"I know. But puppies go to their new owners at about eight weeks, and people don't just turn up and take a puppy home. We'll have to let them come and see the puppies – and we need to meet them to make sure we like them." She hugged Lauren. "We're not going to give Bella's lovely pups to just anyone, sweetheart, don't worry."

Lauren nodded. "But – but not Lucy?" she asked quickly. "She isn't big enough yet, Mum."

Mum nodded thoughtfully. "You're probably right. Lucy will have to be a bit older than the others when she goes. Not much though, I shouldn't think. You've done so well feeding her, she's catching them up." She looked at Lauren. "I know you really love Lucy, and it'll be hard for you to say goodbye, but you'll still have Bella, remember."

Lauren buried her nose in Buster's soft fur. She loved Bella, of course she did. But Lucy would have died if Lauren hadn't woken up that first night. It felt like she and Lucy belonged together. But Lauren just didn't think she could explain that to Mum.

She put Buster back in the puppy pen, and ran upstairs to fetch Lucy. When she opened her bedroom door, Lucy scrabbled at the side of the box with her claws, squeaking frantically.

"Oh, I'm sorry. I went off and left you, didn't I?" Lauren scooped up the puppy, her eyes filling with tears. "I didn't mean to." She sighed, feeling Lucy wriggle and squirm against her neck. "I don't ever want to leave you. But I'm not going to, am I? You're going to leave me. Oh, Lucy, I don't want you to go!"

The summer holidays seemed to have gone by so quickly, Lauren thought. She could hardly believe there was less than a week to go until school started! She supposed it was because she'd been busy all the time looking after Lucy and Bella, and the other puppies.

Lucy's brothers and sisters loved the little outdoor run that Lauren's dad had made for them, and spent lots of time out there now. Lauren's mum had put a photo of them all romping about on the grass on the pet website where she was advertising them to new owners.

Lauren wasn't sure about letting Lucy go out in the run yet – she was still so much littler than the other puppies, and Lauren was worried that they might hurt her with their rough and tumble games.

"Mum, can I take Lucy out to play in the orchard, if I'm really careful not to let her run off?"

Her mum put down the phone. "Yes, that's fine. Although I'm sure she'd be all right in the run with the others, you know. She's a lot bigger now."

Lauren sighed. She supposed Lucy was catching up. But she still wouldn't feed from Bella like they did. Dad said she liked her special bottles too much. They wouldn't have to do the bottle feeds for too much longer, though. Now that the puppies were five weeks old, they were all having solid food too. Lauren loved to watch them all eating.

The first few meals had gone everywhere but into the puppies' mouths, and Bella had ended up having most of it as she'd licked it off the puppies. They had the same dry food as Bella, but mixed with the puppy milk Lucy had, and they always ended up with mush caked all over their ears.

"Who was on the phone?" Lauren asked, as she finished her toast. "It wasn't someone about the puppies, was it?"

"No, it was just Nicky, Sam's mum. We'd talked about sharing the school run next week, and she wanted to know if we'd rather do morning or afternoon. I said we'd pick you up in the afternoon, is that OK? I like hearing about your day."

Lauren gaped at her. "Sam's going to my school?" she asked.

"Well, of course he is. Yours is the only school close by."

"He's not in my class, is he?"

"No, he's in the other class in your year." Her mum frowned. "His mum and I talked about it when they came round, didn't you hear us?"

Lauren shook her head. She supposed she'd been too busy being grumpy about having to entertain Sam. And now she had to share lifts to school with him! She knew it would make less work for Mum and Dad, but she didn't want to share her car journeys; she liked having the time to chat to them.

Crossly, she picked up Lucy and

a ball from the puppy pen and stomped out into the yard.

Lucy squirmed excitedly in Lauren's arms, sniffing all the interesting new smells. She'd been everywhere in the house with Lauren, but this was different. A butterfly fluttered past, and she yapped at it in delight. When they got to the orchard, which had a brick wall all round it, Lauren gently put her down on the grass.

Lucy looked up at her, not sure what she was supposed to do. She gave an enquiring little whine.

"Go play!" Lauren rolled the ball, and Lucy chased after it, yapping. She tried to sink her teeth into it, but it was just too big, and she ended up rolling over on top of the ball with a squeak of dismay.

Lucy bounced up and went off sniffing around in the grass, until she came to a dock plant, with big shield-shaped leaves. She licked a leaf thoughtfully, and then seized it in her teeth, pulling hard. It sprang back, and she jumped around yapping fiercely, until Lauren nearly choked with laughter.

All of a sudden there was a heavy thud, and a big football bounced over the orchard wall and thumped on to the grass right next to Lucy, who whimpered in fright. She scampered over to Lauren.

Lauren snatched Lucy up in one arm, grabbed the ball with the other and ran across to the wall, to find Sam peering over it.

"Hey! You almost hit Lucy with that! What are you doing?" Lauren snapped.

"Sorry! I was just kicking the ball around..." Sam looked guilty.

"You could have hurt her!" Lauren told him, as she shoved the ball into his hands.

"Sorry..." Sam muttered again, and he walked away with his shoulders hunched up.

Lauren almost felt sorry for telling him off, but then Lucy wriggled into her neck, whimpering, and Lauren felt cross all over again.

When school started the next week, Lauren had to share lifts with Sam, as her mum had arranged, but Lauren hardly talked to him. She didn't really know what to say, and Sam seemed shy of her. She supposed it was because of the way she'd told him off in the orchard.

It was great being back at school and seeing all her friends again, but she really missed Lucy and the other puppies.

"Are they big enough for new homes yet?" Millie asked, at break.

"Mum's got people coming to see them already, and they can leave Bella after next week, she says. People have already chosen six of them. Not Lucy, though, she's still too little." *Thank goodness*, she added silently. At the weekend, a family had come to see the puppies, and the little girl had picked up Lucy, saying she wanted her. Lauren had felt sick watching. Luckily, Mum had seen her horrified face, and explained that Lucy was too little to go for a few more weeks. The family had chosen two girl puppies named Daisy and Danni instead. But afterwards Mum had sat down with Lauren and hugged her, and explained that she was going to have to let Lucy go sometime.

"You'll really miss her, won't you?" Millie said, putting her arm through Lauren's, and Lauren nodded.

"Couldn't you ask your mum and dad if you can keep her?" Millie suggested.

"I wish I could," Lauren whispered. "They've always said we can't, that we already have Bella. But I just can't bear to think of Lucy belonging to someone else."

Chapter Six

Lucy watched the strange boy cuddling Buster and wondered who he was. There were lots of other people in her kitchen too, but they all seemed friendly. Everyone who had come to the house over the last two weeks had wanted to stroke her and her brothers and sisters, and play with them. It was fun, but it was confusing too. She had a feeling that this boy was going to take Buster away. He had been before, and this time he had picked Buster up straight away, and Buster had wagged his tail and yipped happily, the way Lucy did when Lauren cuddled her.

If Buster went away with this boy, then she would be the only puppy left. Daisy and Danni had gone with a little girl the day before. The girl's mother had put them in a special box with a wire front, and Lauren had taken her out to see Daisy and Danni drive off in a car. Lauren had hugged her extra tight, and seemed really sad, although she'd cheered up and giggled when Lucy licked her ear.

Lucy missed rolling over and over with all the others, now that it was just her and Buster. She still had Lauren to play with, of course, and that was her favourite thing. But was she going to go somewhere too, like all her brothers and sisters? She didn't want to. She wanted to stay here with Lauren.

The boy snuggled Buster under his chin, and then turned to put him into a carrier like the one Daisy and Danni went away in. Lucy watched them go out into the yard, and then she looked around the puppy run, with its rumpled blankets and scattered toys, and howled a big beagle howl.

"Oh! Did Buster go today?" Lauren asked in surprise when she got home – she had been to Millie's house for tea.

"Yes, it's only Lucy left," her mum answered. "Did you have a good time?"

"Yes, it was great," Lauren replied, only half listening. She was looking at Lucy curled up asleep on the fluffy bed at one side of the puppy run. She seemed so tiny and alone.

Lucy woke up and stared around her at the empty run, looking confused. She let out a tiny whimper, and staggered to her feet, sniffing around the pen. Bella leaned over and licked her gently, and Lucy stopped whimpering, but she still looked uncertain.

Mum put her arm around Lauren. "She's got so much bigger, hasn't she? And you can really see all the brown coming out on her now. She's going to be so beautiful. You did really well with the hand-rearing, Lauren, it was such hard work. Dad and I are very proud of you, you know."

"Thanks," Lauren muttered. She was proud of what she'd managed with Lucy too, but she had a horrible feeling that she knew what was coming next.

"I know you'll miss her, sweetheart, but she's ready to go to a new home, isn't she?" Mum said gently. "She's hardly bothering with her bottles, and she's having dry food now."

Lauren nodded, and sniffed. It was all true, but that didn't make it any easier. She pulled away from her mum with a muttered, "Sorry!", picked up Lucy, who squeaked in surprise, and fled upstairs.

Lauren was really looking forward to Friday and the start of the weekend. She enjoyed being back at school, but she missed Lucy so much – and she wasn't sure how much more time they had together.

Her dad had picked up her and Sam as usual, and they sat in the back seat while Dad tried to ask cheerful questions about how Sam was settling in, and Sam kept saying things like, "OK," and, "Fine thanks."

They dropped Sam off, and then Lauren ran inside to say hello to Lucy.

The phone was ringing as she went into the kitchen, and her mum yelled from upstairs, "Can you answer that, Lauren? I'm just making the beds!"

Lauren grabbed the phone, hoping it wasn't an order for her parents' camping supplies company, as she always worried she'd get them wrong.

"Hello?"

"Is that Mrs Woods? With the beagle puppies?"

"Oh! Yes – I mean, I'm her daughter," Lauren explained.

"Oh good. Do you have any puppies left? I've only just seen the website."

Lauren swallowed. This lady might end up being Lucy's owner. All of a sudden her eyes filled with tears. "There is one puppy left," she said, making her voice sound very doubtful.

"Right – is there something wrong with it?" the lady on the phone sounded worried.

"We-ell... She was the smallest of the litter, you see, much smaller than the others. We had to hand-rear her."

"Oh dear. Well, if she's not healthy I think I'll try someone else. Thanks, anyway."

Lauren pressed the button to end the call with a shaky hand, and put down the phone.

But she couldn't answer the phone every time someone called...

Still feeling really guilty, Lauren took Lucy out into the garden to play. She threw a ball for Lucy to chase, and she raced up and down the garden with excited squeaks.

"Lauren!" Mum was calling from the little bit of garden round the side of the house, where the washing line was. "Can you help me hang the washing out, please?"

Lauren sighed. Hanging out the washing was one of the jobs she did to earn her allowance. "Sorry, Lucy," she said, picking her up. "You go in the run, OK? Back soon."

Lucy stared after her, whining. Lauren had left the ball on the grass, and there were no toys in the run. Lucy ran up and down, sniffing at the wire, then scratched at it, wondering if she could get out and fetch the ball. She stuck a small paw through the wire fence, but the ball was too far away to reach.

Yapping crossly, Lucy scratched at the wire again, standing up on her hind paws. Her claws caught in the wire. She looked at them thoughtfully, and unhooked them. Then she stretched up higher, clinging on tight. She was climbing! Wriggling and scrambling, she worked her way up the side of the run. She teetered on the top, not quite sure what to do next. All at once, she let go and scrambled down the other side, landing in a little heap.

She sprang up and shook herself excitedly. There it was – her ball! She chased after it, scrabbling it along with her front paws, and followed the ball as it rolled through the garden gate, and out into the yard.

Ten minutes later, Lauren dashed back, eager to go on playing with Lucy, only to find that Lucy wasn't there.

She stood staring at the run. The fence was about thirty centimetres high – surely Lucy was far too little to climb out?

"Lucy! Lucy!" Lauren cried, as she ran all round the run.

But the little puppy was nowhere to be seen.

Chapter Seven

Lucy pattered across the yard, and set off exploring around the other side of the orchard wall. She'd abandoned the ball in favour of all the other interesting things she could smell. Perhaps she'd find Lauren if she went down here, too. She spotted a snail climbing up the wall and watched it round-eyed. She went closer and sniffed. It had an odd smell, and she decided it wasn't for eating.

"Hey! Lucy!" Lucy jumped, and looked up. That wasn't Lauren's voice.

It was the boy, Sam, holding a big ball. She'd seen him before when he came to the house to fetch Lauren in the mornings. She sniffed his fingers in a friendly sort of way. Maybe he would play with her?

"Are you supposed to be out here on your own?" he asked. "I bet you're not."

"Lucy! Lucy!" There was a distant voice calling, sounding worried.

"You're definitely not," Sam told Lucy. "That sounds like Lauren looking for you."

Lucy could hear Lauren too, but she wasn't quite sure where she was. She whimpered anxiously.

"It's OK. Let's find Lauren, yes?" Sam looked down at her, and Lucy pawed his foot eagerly.

"Come on then. Good girl," Sam put down the ball, and picked up Lucy. He walked quickly down to the yard. "Hey, Lauren, I've got her!"

Lauren came dashing out of the garden gate. She grabbed Lucy, hugging her tightly while Lucy whined with delight. "Oh, you star, Sam! I was really worried. She must have climbed out of her run. Thanks!"

"Beagles are really good at escaping." Sam nodded, and Lauren looked at him in surprise. "I really like dogs," he explained. "We can't have one, because Dad's allergic, but I've got loads of dog books. And I once saw a video on a website of a beagle climbing out of a massive pen."

"Oh." Lauren suddenly felt really ashamed. She'd been going to school with Sam every day, and she hadn't asked him anything about himself, or said a single friendly thing. "It's brilliant that you found her. What if she'd gone on to the road?"

Sam nodded. "I can't imagine losing a dog like that," he agreed. "It would be awful."

Lauren's eyes suddenly welled up.

"Sorry! I didn't mean to make you cry!" Sam said, looking horrified.

"It's OK," Lauren gulped. "It's just – you don't understand…" She wiped her hand across her eyes, while Lucy licked at her cheek anxiously.

"Lucy isn't mine. Not for ever. She's going to have a new home, just like the other puppies. And I can't bear the thought of not having her any more."

"Oh wow," Sam muttered. "I thought you were keeping her, when she stayed and all the others went. And she's with you all the time."

"I've always known she'd have to go, like her brothers and sisters," Lauren whispered. "I still have Bella, and of course I love her, but I've spent so much time with Lucy, because we hand-reared her. It's going to be awful when she leaves. It was bad enough when people came for the others, but Lucy's special." She opened the orchard gate, and gently shooed Lucy in. "Want to come and play with her?" she said.

Sam nodded and followed her. "Has anyone come to see Lucy?" he asked.

Lauren shook her head. "Someone rang earlier, and I sort of mentioned how Lucy was the runt of the litter and made this lady think she wasn't very well…"

She glanced at Sam, not sure what he'd think, but Sam looked impressed.

"I felt really guilty afterwards," Lauren admitted. "And I can't keep putting people off."

Sam looked thoughtful. "There must be something you can do. I'll help you." He looked at Lucy, who was destroying a windfall apple. "You can't lose her," he said firmly.

Lauren smiled. He sounded so certain it made her feel a little bit better.

The next morning, Sam knocked at the kitchen door while Lauren was finishing her breakfast, and slipping cornflakes to Bella and Lucy, who were sitting on either side of her chair.

"Morning, Mrs Woods," he said politely to Lauren's mum. "Um, I was just wondering if Lauren wanted to come out and play."

"I'm sure she does!" Lauren's mum said, looking delighted, and Lauren rolled her eyes at Sam, who tried not to laugh.

"I'm popular then," he said quietly, as they went across the yard with Lucy and Bella on their leads.

"Mum thinks it's really nice for me to

have a friend living close by." Lauren swallowed nervously. "Sorry I haven't been very friendly. I was a bit cross when Mum arranged the lifts and everything – like I didn't have a choice."

"Me too!" Sam agreed. "My mum kept going on about how lucky I was, and I was like, she's a girl and I've never even met her! Sorry," he added. "Anyway, I've got a plan!"

"You have?" Lauren asked eagerly. "Tell me."

Sam sat down on the rusty old tractor that had been abandoned on the edge of the field and beamed. "I think we should buy Lucy ourselves! I've got thirty pounds of birthday money left. I'd give you that, no problem, if I could sort of share Lucy. Take her for walks sometimes and stuff. It's the closest I'll get to having a dog, after all."

Lauren nodded slowly. "I've got the money my gran gave me at the beginning of the holidays, but I've been so busy with the puppies I never got round to spending it. That's fifty pounds so far. Puppies can't cost more than a hundred pounds, can they? But how are we going to find the rest of the money?"

Sam grinned. "I thought we could pick the apples from the orchard, and sell them. We could set up a stall on that big patch of grass where the lane down to the farm ends. It's close enough to the road for people to see us and stop."

Lauren jumped off the tractor wheel. "That's a brilliant idea! Mum and Dad never have time to pick them, they won't mind. I'll go and get some buckets."

It took a while to pick the apples, as a lot of them had wasps in, and had to be thrown on the compost heap, but eventually they had three buckets of really nice-looking ones. Lauren grabbed a handful of freezer bags from the kitchen, when they went back home for lunch, and Sam found an old folding table in the big shed at the back of the cottage, and he borrowed one of the boxes from the move to make into cardboard signs.

Then Lauren had another brainwave. "You start selling the apples. I've just remembered, Mum's always saying I ought to clear out my old soft toys. We can sell those, too. Here, you take

Lucy, I'm going to sneak back home and get them."

By the time she struggled down the lane with a bin bag full of bears and dogs, Sam was looking very pleased with himself. "I've sold three bags! That's one pound fifty!" He'd made the signs as well, and tied a couple on to the hedges on both sides of the road.

apples
50p

"Brilliant! Help me put out the toys on the grass at the front of the table. They're bound to make people look."

"Lucy and Bella have been making people stop too, they've had loads of petting."

It turned out the toys were almost more popular than the apples. Lauren even had to go back and find some more soft toys that she hadn't been planning to get rid of, but she didn't mind giving up her Beanie toy dogs if it meant she could keep her real one.

"How much have we made?" Sam asked, as they packed up at teatime.

"Twenty pounds!" Lauren beamed. "So that's seventy altogether. And there's loads more apples we can pick. But I don't think I've got any more old toys."

Lauren's mum and dad were so pleased she was getting on with Sam that they didn't ask what they'd been doing all afternoon. And they didn't mind at all when she and Sam and the dogs disappeared off again the next morning.

It was the middle of the morning, and they were doing quite well, when a car pulled up by the stall.

"Would you like some apples?" Sam asked, sounding very professional, and the man smiled and dug around in his pockets for some change.

"Actually, I'm looking for Redhills Farm," he explained, as Lauren handed the apples through the car window.

"It's down there." Lauren pointed down the lane.

"Thanks. I've come to look at a beagle puppy – is that the mum? She's beautiful." He nodded at Bella, who was sitting by Lauren's side. He couldn't see Lucy, as she was curled up asleep, half inside Sam's hoodie top.

"Y-yes..." Lauren stammered, and the man waved and drove away.

Sam and Lauren stared at each other in horror. The man had come about Lucy! They were too late!

Chapter Eight

"What are we going to do?" Lauren whispered. "We can't let him have her, we can't! Mum didn't say anyone was coming, he must have just turned up."

Sam nodded. "We've nearly got enough money, as well. It's just not fair."

Lauren looked at him, frowning. "If Lucy's not there, he can't see if he likes her..." she suggested slowly.

"You mean we should just stay here?" Sam asked.

Lauren shook her head. "No. Because he's seen us, and Mum knows we've got Lucy. We have to hide. Come on!"

"Where are we going?" Sam asked.

"I don't know yet. Let's just get away from here."

"OK." Sam zipped up his hoodie, and used it like a bag to carry Lucy, while Lauren grabbed Bella's lead.

Lucy woke up as they ran back down the lane, as Sam was jiggling her around inside his top. She gave an indignant squeak, and tried to wriggle out.

Lauren turned back. "I'll take her, she'll be quieter with me. Shhh, Lucy!" Lucy snuggled gratefully into Lauren's arms, as Sam handed her over.

As they peered round the corner of the barn, they saw the man's car parked in the yard. The top half of the back door was open and they could see him talking to Lauren's mum in the kitchen.

"Let's hide in the barn," Lauren said quickly. "If we go behind the bales of straw, we'll still be able to see if they come out."

They sneaked through the open doors, and settled themselves at the back of the barn.

"Shhh! I can hear my mum," Lauren whispered.

"Lauren! Lauren!" They could just see Lauren's mum, looking a bit embarrassed. "She's probably in the orchard, playing with Lucy," she said.

"I'm sorry, I should've called first," the man said. "I saw the ad and thought I'd just drop in, as I was coming this way. There were two children up at the top of the lane with a beagle."

"Oh! Well, that would be Lauren and Sam. I hope they haven't gone along the road, Lauren knows not to. I'd better go up there and find them. You stay here and drink your tea."

Lauren sank back behind the straw bales. "She's going to be upset when she finds we aren't there," she said slowly.

"Do you want to let your mum know where we are?" Sam asked.

Lauren chewed her lip uncertainly, but then Lucy woke up again inside Sam's hoodie and wriggled out. She gave a little yap, and looked up at Lauren with her big brown eyes. She looked so gorgeous that Lauren knew she couldn't bear to let her go. "No," she said firmly. "He'll give up waiting soon, hopefully."

Lucy climbed off Lauren's lap and went sniffing round the floor, and nudging up against Bella, who was sensibly curled up on a pile of straw. Bella yawned and licked Lucy half-heartedly. It looked like she just wanted to sleep.

Lucy could smell delicious smells all

round the barn. She pattered off round the edge of the bale to investigate, and Lauren and Sam both dived to grab her, which made Bella bark.

"Ssshhh!" Lauren hissed, putting her finger to her lips, and Bella gave her a confused look. "Sorry, Bella, sweetie. But we have to be quiet, OK?"

Sam put Lucy in his lap, and started to wave a piece of straw for her to chase. "I don't think we can keep this little one quiet, though," he said, as Lucy squeaked delightedly and growled at the straw.

"They might not hear from out there. Oh, there's Mum. She looks a bit worried," Lauren said guiltily.

Lauren's mum went into the house, and obviously told the man she couldn't find Lauren and Lucy, because he came out and got into his car.

"I'm so sorry," Lauren's mum said.

Lauren thought the man looked disappointed, but she was more worried about the anxious look on her mum's face.

The man handed Lauren's mum a bit of paper. "Here's my phone number, anyway. If you could give me a ring." Then he drove off down the lane.

Lucy growled at the straw again. Sam had stopped waving it about, and she was getting bored. She whined loudly, and tugged the hem of Lauren's jeans with her teeth. She wanted them to play properly.

"Should we come out, now he's gone?" Sam asked.

Lauren wanted to, especially as she could hear her mum calling for her dad, who was working in the office at the back of the house. Now they'd both be searching for her. But she shook her head. "What if they just call the man to come back?" She nibbled her nails. "I think we have to give it a bit longer."

They could hear Lauren's mum and dad going round the house shouting her name. Finally, Bella started whining. "I know, Bella," Lauren whispered. "I'm hungry too."

"I'm starving," Sam muttered, and then he gasped as he heard a different voice. "That's my mum!"

Sam's mum came running into the yard carrying Molly. Molly was crying and calling, "Sam?"

Sam and Lauren exchanged a guilty glance.

"I'm sorry, I'll have to go out. Molly looks really upset…" Sam was getting to his feet. "You stay, I'll say I wasn't with you."

"It's OK, I'm coming too," Lauren told him. "And I promise you won't get into trouble. I'll say it was all my idea." They crept over to the barn door, and peered out anxiously. Bella looked round their legs, unsure what was going on. Only Lucy was happy, and squeaked excitedly to see everyone.

"Sam!"

"Lauren!"

"Didn't you hear us calling you? We've been shouting for ages!" Lauren's mum hugged her. "We had no idea where you were!"

Molly struggled down from her mum's arms and ran to hug Sam.

"Were you in the barn the whole time?" Dad asked, looking from Lauren to Sam and back again.

"Um, yes…" Lauren admitted.

"So you were hiding on purpose," Dad said.

Lauren glanced worriedly at Sam, and then said, very fast, "That man had come to buy Lucy, and I didn't want him to."

Mum blinked. "He was very nice. He already has one beagle, and wanted another. He was really disappointed when we couldn't find you."

"Sam, I can't believe you frightened us all like that," his mum said crossly.

"I think we'd all better go inside," Dad said firmly. "I want to understand what's going on here." He shooed Sam and Lauren and the two dogs into the kitchen, where Bella and Lucy went eagerly to their food bowls. "Sit down, you two. Right. Explain. What was wrong with that man that made you decide to do something so silly? He seemed like he'd be a really good owner."

"Nothing…" Lauren began haltingly.

"It wasn't him," Sam put in. "We didn't want anyone to have Lucy. Look." He dug in his hoodie pocket and brought out the old pencil case he'd been keeping the money in.

"Eighty-four pounds," Lauren said proudly, as he emptied it on to the table.

Dad frowned. "I don't get it."

"We were going to buy Lucy ourselves!" Lauren explained. "I really, really don't want to sell her to some stranger! We thought a puppy probably costs about a hundred pounds, and we were so close to having it, and then that man came! We had to hide Lucy away in case he got her first!"

"Is this something to do with the table full of apples at the top of the lane?" Mum asked.

Lauren nodded. "We sold the apples from the orchard, and my old toys, too."

"And it's my birthday money."

"And my money from Grandma."

"There's more apples left," Sam added. "We should get to a hundred, easily."

Mum smiled sadly. "That man was going to pay four hundred pounds. That's what a pedigree puppy costs."

"Four hundred!" Lauren whispered in horror. "We couldn't raise that much. Oh no…" And she started to cry. She was going to have to give Lucy up after all.

Lucy looked up from her bowl. What

was the matter with Lauren? She dashed across the kitchen floor, and scrabbled frantically at Lauren's legs.

Lauren reached down and picked Lucy up, cuddling her close, while Sam stroked her head.

Lucy howled loudly, joining in with Lauren's sobbing.

"Lauren, shhh..." her dad said gently. "And please tell Lucy to hush too, I can't hear myself think. That's better," he added, as Lauren stroked Lucy and shushed her. "We didn't realize you were that desperate to keep Lucy. Why didn't you say?"

"I tried!" Lauren burst out. "But you kept saying we had Bella, and ever since the puppies came you'd said we couldn't keep them. I told Sam about it, didn't I?"

Sam nodded. "But we thought if we had enough money we could keep her. Lauren said I could share her too."

"Oh, Sam…" his mum said sadly. "He loves dogs," she explained to Lauren's parents. "But his dad is allergic."

Lauren's mum was watching Lucy, snuggling up in Lauren's arms, her eyes switching from person to person, as she tried to follow what was going on. "She is lovely," Mum said slowly.

Lauren's dad looked round at her. "It was you that said no more dogs, Annie!"

"Somehow I can't imagine being back to just one, after all those puppies. It already seems very quiet, with only Bella and Lucy." Mum smiled. "And she's definitely the prettiest of the litter."

"So can we keep her?" Lauren asked, not quite sure whether that was what her mum was saying. "Really? You mean it?"

Mum nodded, and laughed as Lauren hugged her, squidging Lucy in between them. "Don't squash her!"

"But if Bella has puppies again, we're not keeping any!" Dad said sternly.

Lauren shook her head. "Oh no, I promise I wouldn't even ask!"

"You can have your birthday money back, Sam," Lauren's mum said, smiling.

Sam nodded, but he looked a bit sad.

"Do you still want to share Lucy, though?" Lauren asked, holding Lucy out to him.

Sam nodded eagerly, and Lucy

wagged her tail so fast it almost blurred, and then licked his hand lovingly.

"We can use the apple money to buy her a really smart new collar and lead," Lauren suggested. "Not Bella's old ones any more. And we can put 'This dog belongs to Lauren and Sam' on her collar tag."

Everyone laughed, and Lucy howled again, a real show-off howl with her ears thrown back and her tail wagging under Sam's arm.

Sam grinned. "I think she likes that idea.

Coming soon:

Smudge the Stolen Kitten

Holly Webb